MAY 3:
Double D-Day. More protesters are arrested, most of whom are under eighteen. Commissioner Bull Connor authorizes the use of high-pressure water hoses and police dogs to control the crowds. Close to one thousand are arrested.

MAY 4–9:
Protests escalate as more adults join the marches. The jails are at maximum capacity, with thousands of young people imprisoned.

MAY 10:
Dr. King and other protest organizers reach an agreement with city leaders that begins the process of desegregation. The Ku Klux Klan holds a rally, and the home of A. D. King, Dr. King's brother, is bombed.

MAY 19:
The school board expels many of the student demonstrators, but a federal judge overturns the expulsions just three days later.

LET THE CHILDREN MARCH

By Monica Clark-Robinson
Illustrated by Frank Morrison

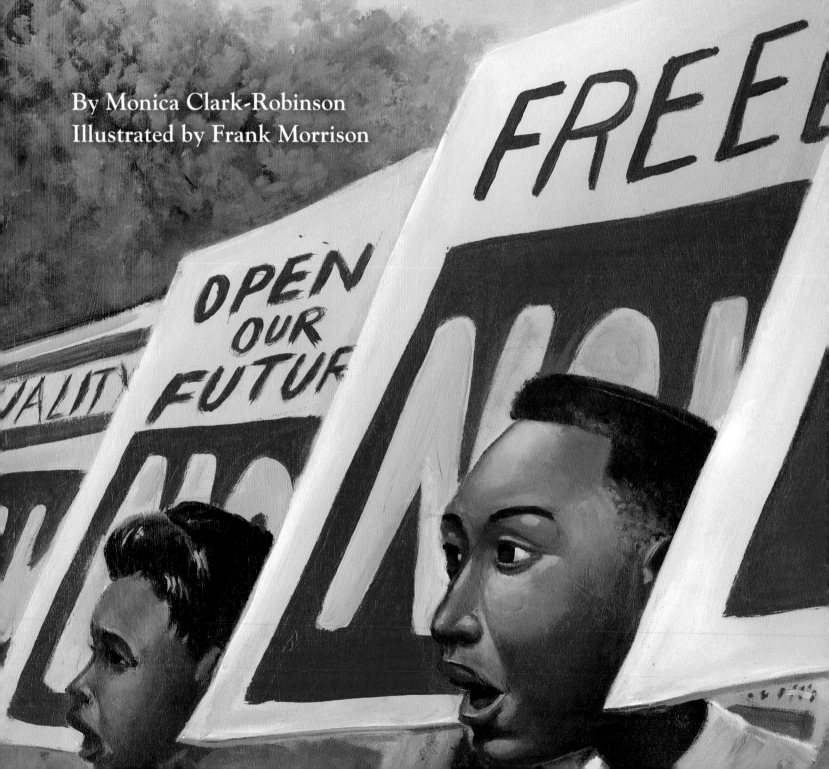

HOUGHTON MIFFLIN HARCOURT

Boston   New York

For the children and teens of Birmingham, Alabama, 1963 —M.C.-R.

To my children, who continue to honor our past and our ancestors with their tenacity, ambition, audacity, intelligence, charm, and artistry while becoming the best they can be and then some. —F.M.

Library of Congress Cataloging-in-Publication Data
Names: Clark-Robinson, Monica, author. | Morrison, Frank, 1971– illustrator.
Title: Let the children march / by Monica Clark-Robinson ; illustrated by Frank Morrison.
Description: Boston ; New York : Houghton Mifflin Harcourt, [2018] | Summary: Under the leadership of Dr. Martin Luther King, children and teenagers march against segregation in Birmingham, Alabama, in 1963. | Includes bibliographical references.
Identifiers: LCCN 2016014699 | ISBN 9780544704527 (hardcover)
Subjects: | CYAC: Civil rights demonstrations—Fiction. | Segregation—Fiction. | African Americans—Fiction. | Birmingham (Ala.)—History—20th century—Fiction.
Classification: LCC PZ7.1.C585 Le 2018 | DDC [E]—dc23
LC record available at https://lccn.loc.gov/2016014699

1963
BIRMINGHAM, ALABAMA

I couldn't play on the same playground as the white kids.
I couldn't go to their schools.
I couldn't drink from their water fountains.
There were so many things I couldn't do.

One warm spring night, my family went to church.
We weren't there to have regular services.
We were there to hear Dr. King speak.
We were there to plan.

He wanted to raise an army of
peaceful protesters to fight for freedom.
His brown eyes flashing fire and love,
Dr. King told us the time had come to march.

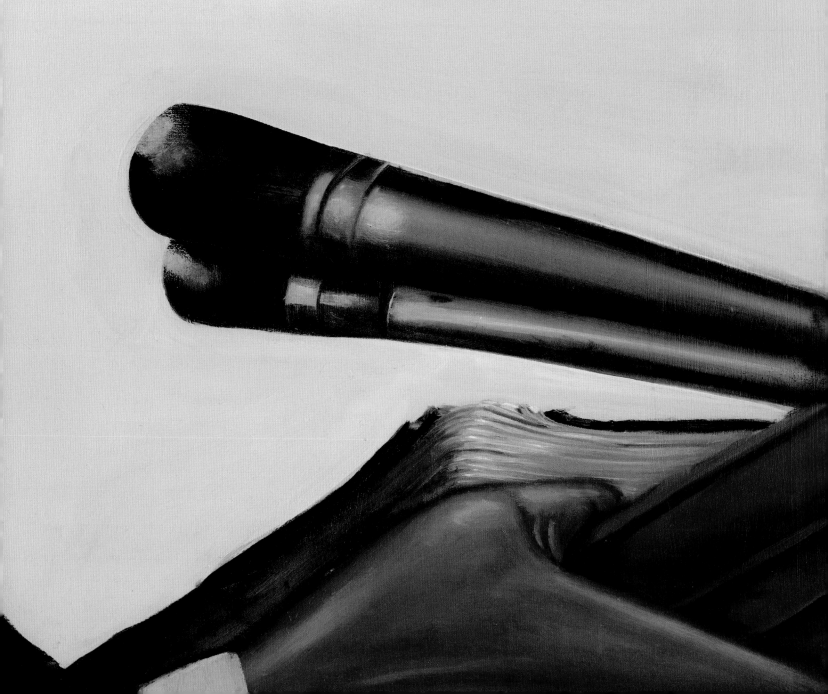

"If I march," Momma said, "I'll lose my job, sure enough."
"I can't march," Daddy said. "I got a family to feed."
The weight of the world rested on our parents' shoulders,
but *this* burden, *this* time, did not have to be theirs to bear.

"I don't have a boss to fear," my brother said, "or a job to lose."
"We can march this time. We'll be Dr. King's army," I said.
"I'll be fine, Daddy," I promised. "Don't worry, Momma."

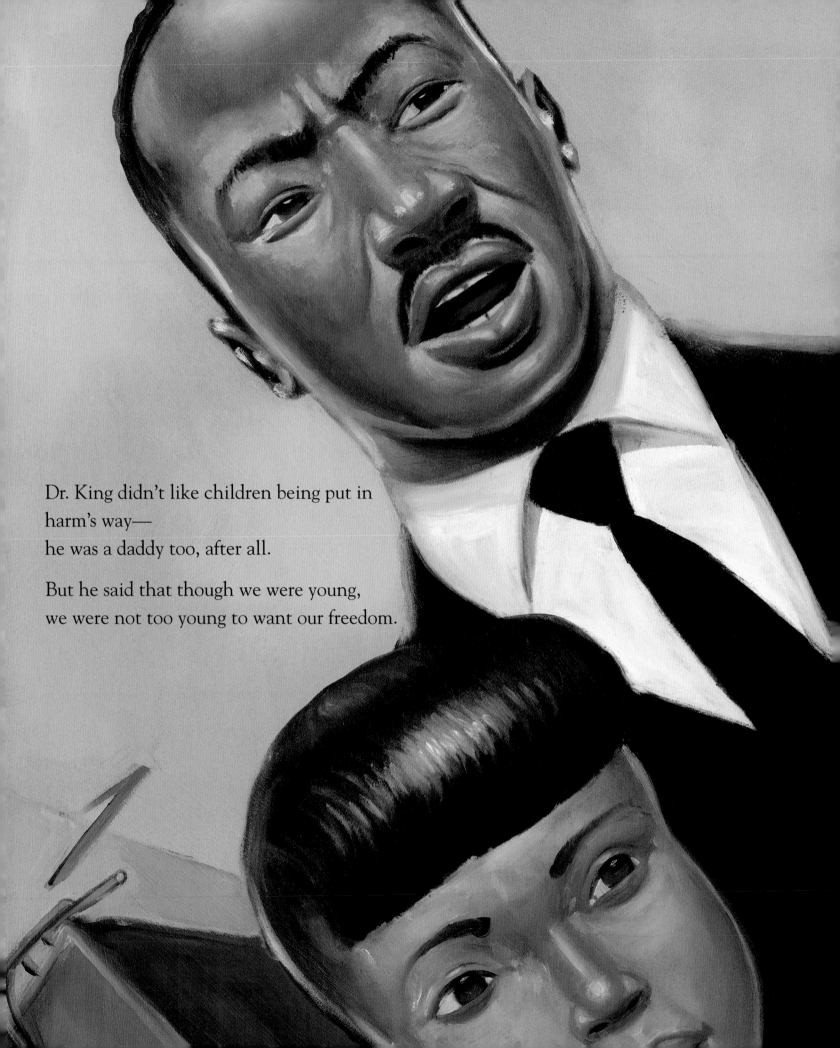

Dr. King didn't like children being put in
harm's way—
he was a daddy too, after all.

But he said that though we were young,
we were not too young to want our freedom.

On May second —a sunny Thursday—
boys and girls, brothers and sisters, cousins and friends,
we all met at the church, dressed in our best, feet ready.

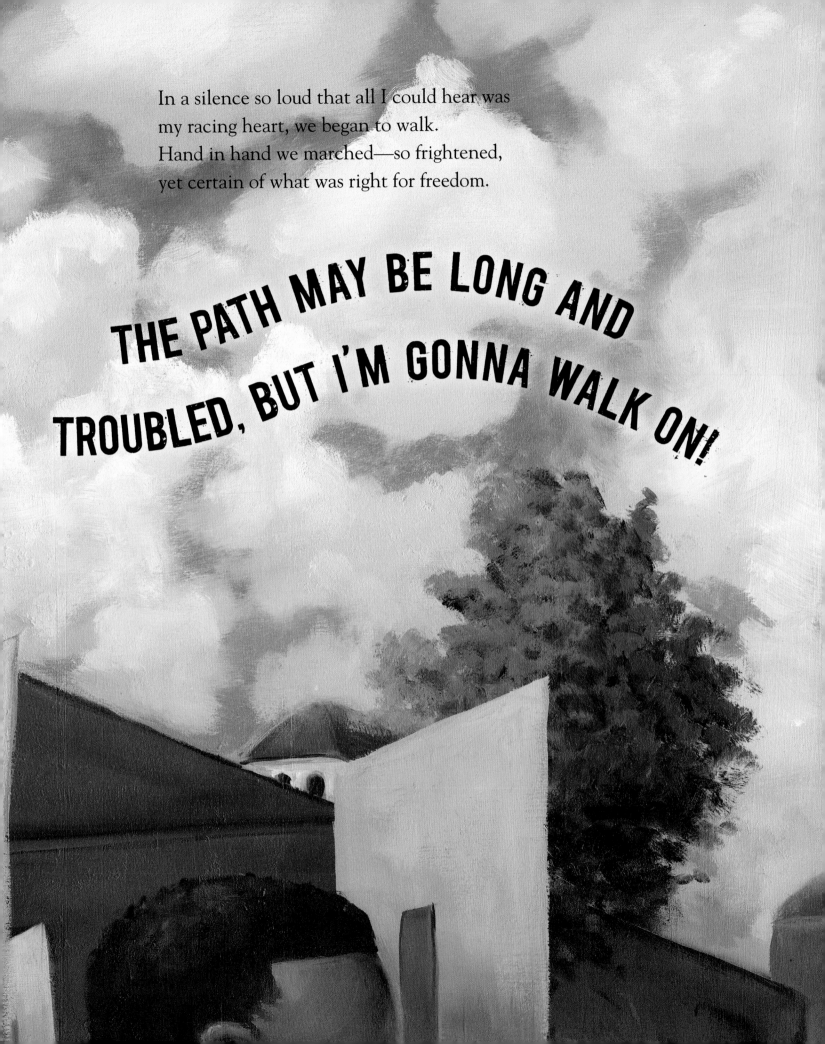

In a silence so loud that all I could hear was
my racing heart, we began to walk.
Hand in hand we marched—so frightened,
yet certain of what was right for freedom.

THE PATH MAY BE LONG AND
TROUBLED, BUT I'M GONNA WALK ON!

Would I be hurt? Would we be heard?
Would it all be worth it in the end?
I wanted to run from the angry faces in the crowd,
run from danger, run from fear.

SINGING THE SONGS OF FREEDOM,

Boys and girls, brothers and sisters, cousins and friends,
on and on we marched,

we marched,

we marched.

ONE THOUSAND STRONG WE CAME.

Hate dogged my heels all that day,
its yellowed canine teeth sharp—
but Courage walked by my side and kept me going.

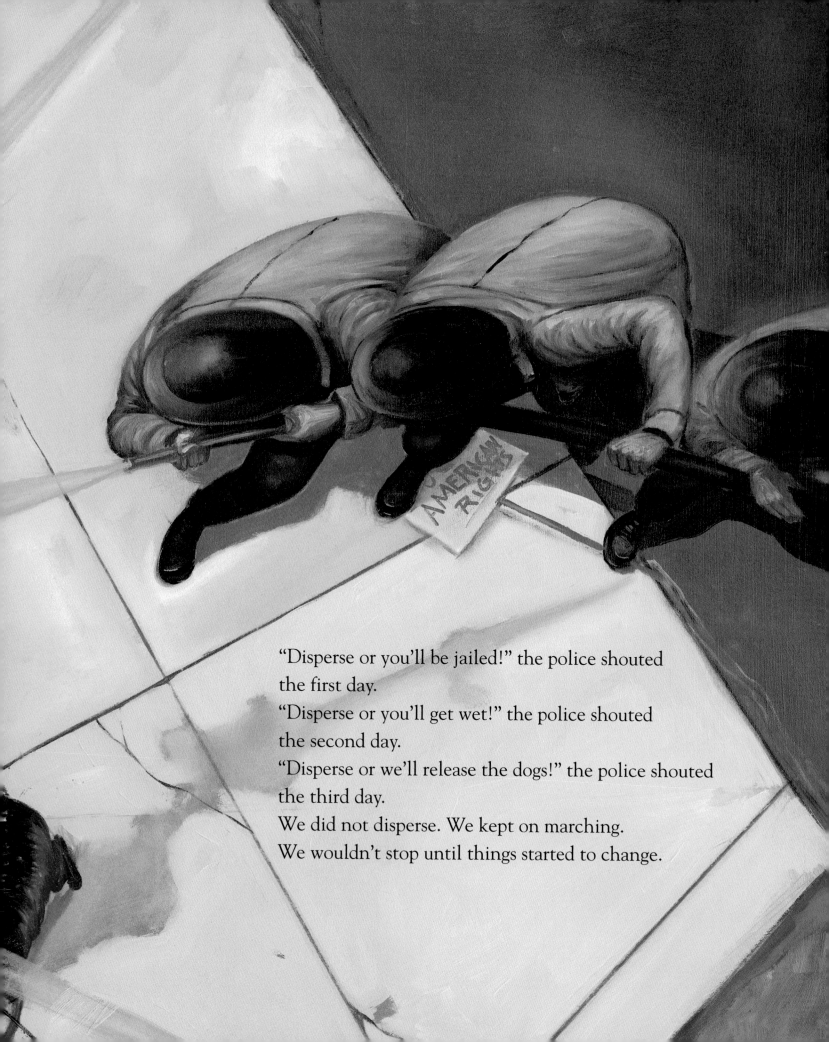

"Disperse or you'll be jailed!" the police shouted
the first day.
"Disperse or you'll get wet!" the police shouted
the second day.
"Disperse or we'll release the dogs!" the police shouted
the third day.
We did not disperse. We kept on marching.
We wouldn't stop until things started to change.

Hundreds of us went to jail on the first day,
and even more on the second.
My turn wasn't until
the third day.

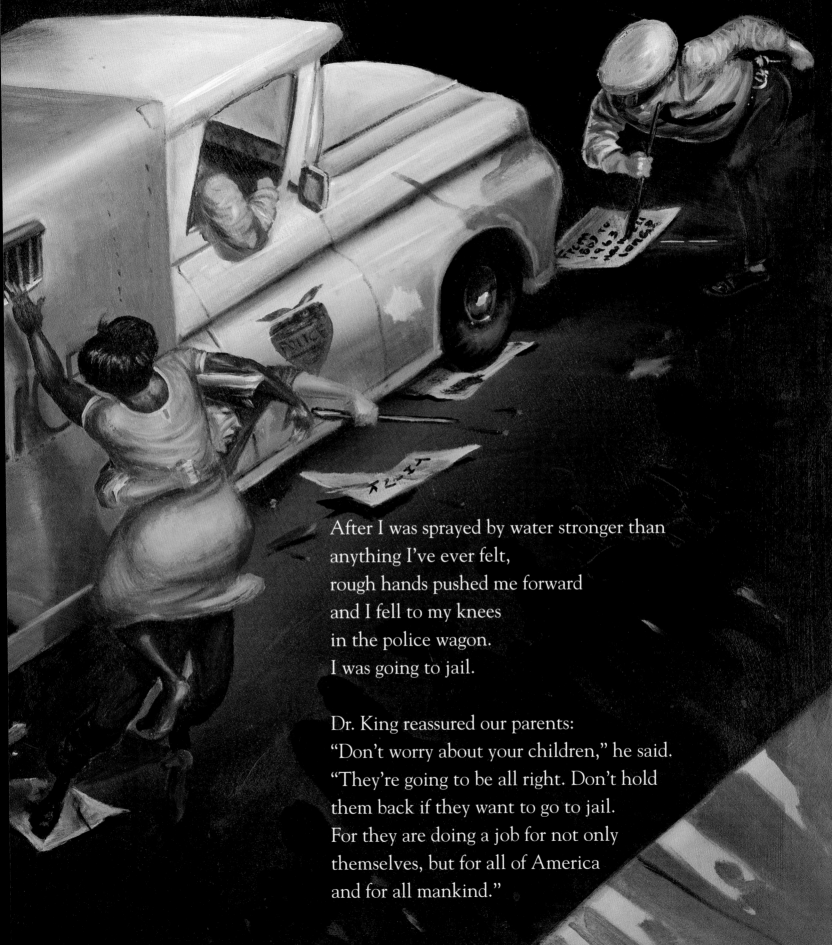

After I was sprayed by water stronger than
anything I've ever felt,
rough hands pushed me forward
and I fell to my knees
in the police wagon.
I was going to jail.

Dr. King reassured our parents:
"Don't worry about your children," he said.
"They're going to be all right. Don't hold
them back if they want to go to jail.
For they are doing a job for not only
themselves, but for all of America
and for all mankind."

That night, crowded into a cell too small
for even half of the kids, we sang:
"We Shall Overcome!"
"Ain't Gonna Let Nobody Turn Me 'Round!"
and "Freedom Is Coming!"
Our parents couldn't be there with us,
but still we sang,
wrapped in the proud and loving
arms of our ancestors.

I was still in jail, but we heard that the next day, and
the next, more kids marched.
The water hoses they used to sting us
could not stop *our* fierce tide.

Turn the other cheek, we had been taught.
Show love where there is hate.
The world watched as Hate bruised us,
but for seven days we walked only in Love.
The jails swelled to bursting,
and even President Kennedy took notice!
Daddy said the president received letters and calls
about us from all over the world.
Our march would become a memory, a small part of a larger story.
But we had been heard, and the seeds of revolution were sown!

Two days and nights I stayed in the jail. Some stayed even longer.
When I left, I was tired and sore, and my best dress was ripped,
but my smile was as wide as the Mississippi River.
I had made a difference.
"I'm so proud of you, baby girl," Mama said.
"Your march was what made them see."
With nothing more than our feet, voices, and courage,
we had done what others could not.
Change was right around the corner;
we felt it like a cool breeze in an Alabama August.
On May 10, the great news rang out:
Dr. King had reached an agreement with the white leaders of the city.
Desegregation would begin.

One month later, I was playing on a playground I'd never
been allowed to play on before.
Two months later, my family ate at a diner we'd never
been allowed to eat in before.
Our march made the difference. We children led the way.

PARK

SINGING THE SONGS OF FREEDOM,

AFTERWORD

The children and teens of Birmingham in 1963 changed the world in ways they could never have imagined. Dr. King later wrote, "Looking back, it is clear that the introduction of Birmingham's children into the campaign was one of the wisest moves we made. It brought a new impact to the crusade, and the impetus that we needed to win the struggle."

President Kennedy went on television the evening of June 11, just one month after the Children's Crusade, to call for civil rights legislation. He said, "Every American ought to have the right to be treated as he would wish to be treated, as one would wish his children to be treated."

The following year, Congress passed the Civil Rights Act of 1964, and Dr. King won the Nobel Peace Prize. The children truly had made a difference.

There are plenty of ways that you can make a difference too—through volunteering, writing elected officials, fundraising, starting a petition, educating yourself. When asked what she thought the message of the Children's Crusade was for today's youth, Janice Kelsey, who was one of the young marchers, had this to say: "I want young people to know that each one has the ability to make a difference in their environment. . . . You just have to have enough courage to evaluate the situation and stand up for what is right."

ARTIST'S STATEMENT

Time paused when I finished reading this manuscript. In that still moment, I looked around my studio, slowly observing sketchpads, oil paint, canvas, brushes, and bookshelves full of reference and children's books. I was reminded of what I have achieved over years of working eleven-hour days. As I walked to my easel to begin sketching thumbnails for this story, I remembered myself as a teenager.

Many Februarys ago, I watched the civil rights movement documentary *Eyes on the Prize* with my parents. I cringed in my chair the first time I saw children being sprayed by hoses. As the years went by, I found myself rewatching the series. Now I watch it with my own children. Each time, I look forward to Martin Luther King Jr.'s profound speeches—they send chills up my spine. After I heard Martin preach, "If a man is called to be a street sweeper, he should sweep streets even as a Michelangelo painted," I don't think I drew or approached art the same way again; it changed me.

I hope my efforts honor the past—the Birmingham Children's Crusade of 1963—and will inspire, influence, and intrigue the future—the next generation. I hope to encourage them to become the very best they can be, not just in February, Black History Month, but every day.

Getty/Michael Ochs Archives/Stringer

Images like this one were on TVs around the country.

QUOTE SOURCES

"Don't worry about your children . . . for all mankind": Dr. Martin Luther King Jr., transcript from a mass meeting in Birmingham, May 6, 1963. Birmingham Civil Rights Institute.*

"Looking back . . . win the struggle": Dr. Martin Luther King, Jr. *Why We Can't Wait* (New York: New American Library, Harper & Row, 1964).

"Every American . . . to be treated": President John F. Kennedy, address to the nation, June 11, 1963.

"Segregation today . . . forever": George Wallace, inauguration address, January 14, 1963.

*This speech by Dr. King is often dated as May 3, but after noticing some confusion with two different mass meetings, I confirmed with the King Center at Stanford that the accurate date is actually May 6.

BIBLIOGRAPHY

Branch, Taylor. *Parting the Waters: America in the King Years, 1954–1963*. New York: Simon and Schuster, 1988.

Carson, Clayborne, et al., editors. *The Eyes on the Prize Civil Rights Reader: Documents, Speeches, and First-Hand Accounts from the Black Struggle*. New York: Penguin Books, 1991.

Kelsey, Janice. Personal interview, August 2015.

Levinson, Cynthia. *We've Got a Job: The 1963 Birmingham Children's March*. Atlanta: Peachtree Publishers, 2012.

Kids in Birmingham 1963. www.kidsinbirmingham1963.org.

Mayer, Robert H. *When the Children March: The Birmingham Civil Rights Movement*. New York: Enslow Publishers, 2008.

Williams, Juan. *Eyes on the Prize: America's Civil Rights Years, 1954–1965*, 25th anniversary edition. New York: Penguin Books, 2013.

Woolfolk, Odessa. Personal interview at the Birmingham Civil Rights Institute, August 2015.

AUTHOR ACKNOWLEDGMENTS

I would like to thank my family, first and always. You guys are just the best!

I could never have finished this book and done all the hard things like staying positive and finding an agent without the amazing ladies of my critique group. Thank you.

To Crescent Dragonwagon, who helped me write through the fear.

To my spectacular agent, Natalie Lakosil: cheers to all our future books together!

And to a girl's best friend, her editor. Thanks, Christine, for being the nicest, smartest first editor an author could have.

Getty/Bettmann

As many as three thousand children and teens were arrested before the conflict ended.

Associated Press/Bill Hudson

"I knew I was going to jail."
—Janice Kelsey

1963 (CONT.)

JUNE 11: President Kennedy goes on television to speak about civil rights, urging Congress to pass legislation.

JULY 23: Birmingham officially withdraws the Segregation Ordinances.

AUGUST 28: Over 250,000 people descend on Washington, D.C., during the March on Washington, where Dr. Martin Luther King Jr. gives his famous "I Have a Dream" speech.

SEPTEMBER 15: The Sixteenth Street Baptist Church in Birmingham is bombed by Klansmen and segregationists, killing four girls and injuring twenty other people.